Judy
LED
THE
WAY

By **Sandy Eisenberg Sasso**

Illustrated by
Margeaux Lucas

In memory of Judith Kaplan Eisenstein, who taught us to sing the songs of our people.

With gratitude to her daughters, Miriam and Ann Eisenstein,
who graciously shared their memories and family photographs.
— S.E.S.

For my sisters, Bernadette and Jean.
— M.L.

The illustrations were created using a combination of
hand painting in gouache and digital art.

Apples & Honey Press
An imprint of Behrman House Publishers
Millburn, New Jersey 07041
www.applesandhoneypress.com

ISBN 978-1-68115-559-3

Text copyright © 2020 by Sandy Eisenberg Sasso
Illustrations copyright © 2020 by Margeaux Lucas

Library of Congress Cataloging-in-Publication Data

Names: Sasso, Sandy Eisenberg, author. | Lucas, Margeaux, illustrator.
Title: Judy led the way / Sandy Eisenberg Sasso ; illustrated by Margeaux
Lucas.
Description: Millburn : Apples & Honey Press, 2020. | Audience: Ages 5-8 |
Audience: Grades 2-3 | Summary: "Judy Kaplan, daughter of Rabbi Mordecai
Kaplan, was the first girl in America to have a bat mitzvah ceremony.
Judy's true story of courage and curiosity will inspire girls to stay
true to themselves and challenge the status quo"-- Provided by
publisher.
Identifiers: LCCN 2019053089 | ISBN 9781681155593 (hardcover)
Subjects: LCSH: Eisenstein, Judith Kaplan, 1909-1996--Juvenile literature.
| Jewish women--United States--Biography--Juvenile literature. | Women
composers--20th century--Biography--Juvenile literature. |
Musicologists--United States--Biography--Juvenile literature.
Classification: LCC ML410.E355 S27 2020 | DDC 780.92 [B]--dc23
LC record available at https://lccn.loc.gov/2019053089

Design by Alexandra N. Segal
Edited by Dena Neusner
Printed in China

1 3 5 7 9 8 6 4 2

1021/B1545/A7

Judy had barely swallowed her first spoonful of chicken soup when she started asking questions.

Why do I have to practice my music scales?

Why do I have to stop biting my nails?

Why do I have to do so many chores?

"It's good for you," Mama said with a sigh, as she added one more matzah ball to everyone's soup. Her sisters groaned. Judy always had a question.

After dinner, as the last flickers of the Sabbath
candles faded, Mama, Papa, Judy's grandmothers,
and her younger sisters gathered around the piano.

Judy's fingers flew across the keyboard as she played
Jewish melodies, and for a moment the questions stopped.
Songs and laughter bounced off
the living-room walls.

The next morning,
Judy sat in the back of the synagogue
with the women. Even as she joined in chanting
the melodies, she was thinking of more questions.
She knew that her papa, who was the rabbi,
would have answers. She squirmed in her seat,
waiting for the service to be over.

That afternoon at lunch, Judy sat at Papa's right side, as she always did. She waited until after the blessings and her first bite of the sweet challah before she started:

Why do men and

Why don't women read the Torah?

Papa, why can't there be more music in the synagogue?

women sit separately?

Do I have to believe in God?

Judy looked at her father to see if he was annoyed, but he just beamed. "Judy, darling, so many good questions."

He tackled the hardest question first. "What does believing in God mean to you?" he asked Judy.

Judy threw her hands up in the air and groaned, "Papaaaa!"

Papa smiled. "When we love and are kind, when we make the world better, there's God. Instead of looking for **where** God is, start thinking about **when** God is."

Papa's answer made sense to her, even though it was like nothing she had ever heard before. She thought, maybe God is when I play my music and sing new songs.

Papa was thinking about Judy's other questions, too. His answer about women reading Torah was also unexpected.

He explained, "Two years ago, women won the right to vote in this country.

"Now more women are working in stores, offices, and hospitals. They are learning to drive, too.

"But not much has changed in the synagogue."
He looked at his daughters and said, "That's not right."

Judy sat up straight. "Of course, Papa! We know as much Hebrew as the boys. We're just as smart. And we can take part in the service just as well!"

Papa looked straight at Judy. "Judy, you're right. We need to change. You're twelve years old— it's time for you to become a bat mitzvah."

Judy nearly dropped the noodle kugel. Had she heard Papa correctly?

Her grandmothers were shocked. Women did not lead services. They did not sit with the men. They did not read Torah. A bat mitzvah ceremony for girls? Unheard of! Unthinkable! It was not tradition!

Judy and her sisters cleared the table as their grandmothers took their tea into the living room. The girls strained their ears to listen.

Their grandmothers were arguing.

"Tell your son, the rabbi, not to do this thing," said Mama's mother.

"No, he won't listen to me. You talk to your daughter," said Papa's mother.

Judy whispered to her sisters, "It's time for things to change." Her sisters agreed. "You **can** do this."

Over the next few days, Judy went to school and completed her assignments as usual. But she couldn't stop thinking about her bat mitzvah. She started biting her nails again.

She had lots of questions.

As soon as she came home, Judy sat at the piano. Nothing could bother her when she was making music.

What will happen when I stand in front of the congregation?

What if the men tell me to sit in the back?

What if everyone thinks like my grandmothers?
What if the women think that I am showing off?
What if something goes wrong?

On the Friday night before her bat mitzvah, Judy's father called her into his study. "Judy," Papa said, "let me hear you chant the blessings before and after the Torah reading."

Judy started to sing, but her voice cracked and her hands perspired. Papa corrected her pronunciation.

Judy took a few deep breaths, closed her eyes, and sang. "That's perfect." Papa's eyes sparkled. "Now here's the passage from Torah that you will read tomorrow in Hebrew and English. Practice tonight."

That was it: one night to rehearse—no more.

Judy opened the book with the Torah verses she was to read. Her heart was pounding. She whispered the words to herself and then said them in a loud voice, the way she would speak in the synagogue. She closed the book.

She climbed into bed and remembered how the shapes of the first Hebrew letters she had learned had been baked into cakes and topped with honey. Hebrew had always been sweet to her.

But this was different. She was going to read before the whole congregation in the synagogue. No woman had ever done that before.

She started twirling her blond hair in knots and fidgeting with her book. Then she took a deep breath, began humming some of her favorite songs, and finally fell asleep.

The next morning,
Judy put on her favorite blue dress and
buckled her patent leather shoes. Then she and her papa,
mama, three younger sisters, and disapproving grandmothers
walked to the brownstone synagogue.

As they entered, Judy's mother reminded her to go sit with the boys and men, up front. Judy hugged her mother; she smelled like comfort and tenderness. She wondered again why men and women sat separately, but she would wait to ask her questions until later.

Judy could hear every heartbeat in her chest as she took her seat. What if people leave when I start to sing? she wondered.

The services began. The familiar words and melodies floated through her, and she relaxed.

Then Papa motioned for Judy to step forward.

She sang the blessings and read the Torah portion her father had given her the night before.

No one made fun of her.
No one walked out.
No one laughed.
No thunder sounded;
no lightning struck.

Everyone, especially Papa,
was beaming. Even her
grandmothers seemed
to approve.

The Torah scroll was returned to the ark.
The service ended.

The tradition of bat mitzvah in the
synagogue had just begun.

Dear Readers,

I wonder how you feel about asking a lot of questions. Is there someone who loves to tackle big questions with you?

I wonder if you have questions about God.

The Kaplan family kept many traditions and changed some. I wonder what traditions you want to keep and if there are any you want to change.

Judy played piano to calm herself when she was feeling worried or anxious. What do you do to help yourself through changes in your life?

Sandy Sasso

Judy at her "second bat mitzvah"

For my family and me, Judy wasn't just a woman who made history; she was also a friend. We heard her lead music in the synagogue, she introduced us to new melodies, and she taught us many songs.

We also studied and learned from Judy's father, Rabbi Mordecai Kaplan, the founder of Reconstructionist Judaism. In 1922, he decided that his eldest daughter, Judy, should become a bat mitzvah. This had never happened in an American synagogue.

It took years for congregations to allow girls to do what Judy did. But many have since followed in her footsteps. Today, in most synagogues, it is common for a girl to become a bat mitzvah, and often girls do much more than Judy did in 1922. They put on a tallit, read directly from the Torah scroll, and help lead the service.

When Judy grew up, she became a musician and was a pioneer in Jewish music. She published the first Jewish songbook for children. We still sing her lyrics to the song "Hanukkah, Oh Hanukkah," which she translated from the Yiddish.

In 1992, on her eighty-second birthday, Judy celebrated a "second bat mitzvah," surrounded by many distinguished Jewish women. She wore a tallit for the first time. That same year, when our daughter Debbie became a bat mitzvah, Judy was a guest of honor. Her message to Debbie was, "Today I am the oldest bat mitzvah and you are the youngest. Remember to celebrate your Judaism with joy!"